Marvin K. Mooney Will you PLEASE GO NOW!

By Dr. Seuss

HarperCollins *Children's Books*

The Cat in the Hat
™ & © Dr. Seuss Enterprises, L.P. 1957
All Rights Reserved

8 10 9 7

ISBN-10: 0-00-716989-2
ISBN-13: 978-0-00-716989-4

© 1972, 2000 by Dr. Seuss Enterprises, L.P.
All Rights Reserved
A Bright and Early Book for Beginning Beginners
Published by arrangement with Random House Inc.,
New York, USA
First published in the UK 1973
This edition published in the UK 2003 by
HarperCollins*Children's Books,*
a division of HarperCollins*Publishers* Ltd
77-85 Fulham Palace Road
London W6 8JB

Visit our website at:
www.harpercollinschildrensbooks.co.uk

Printed and bound in Hong Kong

The
time
has come.

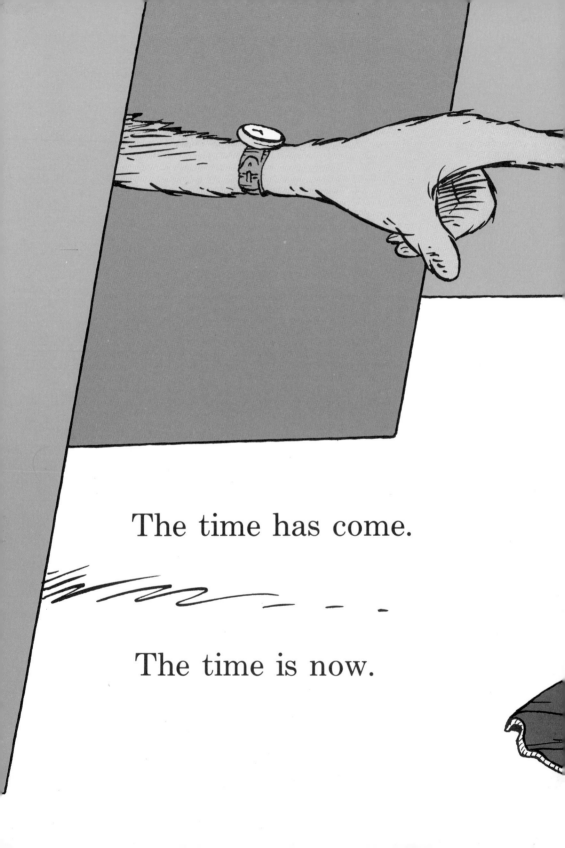

The time has come.

The time is now.

Just go.
Go.
GO!
I don't care how.

You can go by foot.

You can go
by cow.

Marvin K. Mooney,
will you
please go now!

You can go
on skates.

You can go
on skis.

You can go
in a hat.

But
please go.
Please!

I don't care.
You can go
by bike.

You can go
on a Zike-Bike
if you like.

If you like
you can go
in an old blue shoe.

Just go, go, GO!
Please do, do, DO!

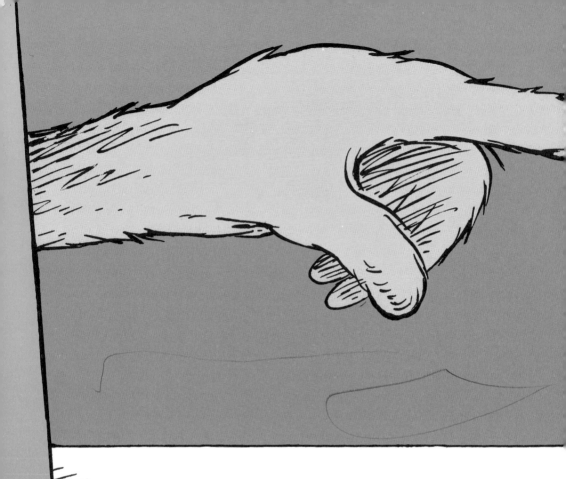

Marvin K. Mooney,
I don't care how.
Marvin K. Mooney,
will you please
GO NOW!

You can go on stilts.

You can go by fish.

You can go
in a Crunk-Car
if you wish.

If you wish
you may go
by lion's tail.

Or stamp yourself
and go by mail.

Marvin K. Mooney!
Don't you know
the time has come
to go, Go, GO!

Get on your way!
Please, Marvin K.!
You might like going
In a Zumble-Zay.

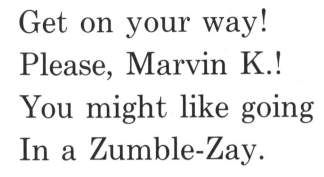

You can go
by balloon ...

... or broomstick.

OR

You can go
by camel
in a
bureau drawer.

You can go by Bumble-Boat . . .

. . . or jet.

I don't care
how you go.

Just GET!

Get yourself a Ga-Zoom.

You can go with a ......

Marvin, Marvin, Marvin!
Will you leave this room!

Marvin K. Mooney!
I don't care HOW.

Marvin K. Mooney!

Will you please

GO NOW!

The time had come.
SO . . .
Marvin WENT.

Dr.Seuss™

The more that you **read,**
the more things **you** will know.
The more that you **learn,**
the **more** places you'll go!

– I Can Read With My Eyes Shut!

With over **30 paperbacks to collect** there's a book for all ages and reading abilities, and now there's never been a better time to have **fun** with **Dr.Seuss!**
Simply collect 5 tokens from the back of each Dr.Seuss book and send in for your

FREE Dr.Seuss poster

(rrp £3.99)

Send your 5 tokens and a completed voucher to:
Dr. Seuss poster offer, PO Box 142, Horsham, UK, RH13 5FJ (UK residents only)

Title: Mr ☐   Mrs ☐   Miss ☐   Ms ☐

First Name: .... Surname: ....

Address: ....

Post Code: .... E-Mail Address: ....

Date of Birth: .... Signature of parent/guardian: ....

TICK HERE IF YOU DO NOT WISH TO RECEIVE FURTHER INFORMATION ABOUT CHILDREN'S BOOKS ☐

Read them **together**, read them **alone**, read them **aloud** and make **reading fun!**
With over **30 wacky stories** to choose from, now it's **easier** than **ever** to find the
right **Dr. Seuss** books for your child – just let the **back cover colour** guide you!

Blue back books
for sharing with your child

Dr. Seuss' ABC
The Foot Book
Hop on Pop
Mr. Brown Can Moo! Can You?
One Fish, Two Fish, Red Fish, Blue Fish
There's a Wocket in my Pocket!

Green back books
for children just beginning to read on their own

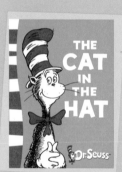

And to Think That I Saw It on Mulberry Street
The Cat in the Hat
The Cat in the Hat Comes Back
Fox in Socks
Green Eggs and Ham
I Can Read With My Eyes Shut!
I Wish That I Had Duck Feet
Marvin K. Mooney Will You Please Go Now!
Oh, Say Can You Say?
Oh, the Thinks You Can Think!
Ten Apples Up on Top
Wacky Wednesday

Yellow back books
for fluent readers to enjoy

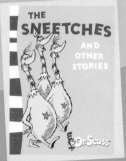

Daisy-Head Mayzie
Did I Ever Tell You How Lucky You Are?
Dr. Seuss' Sleep Book
Horton Hatches the Egg
Horton Hears a Who!
How the Grinch Stole Christmas!
If I Ran the Circus
If I Ran the Zoo
I Had Trouble in Getting to Solla Sollew
The Lorax
Oh, the Places You'll Go!
On Beyond Zebra
Scrambled Eggs Super!
The Sneetches and other stories
Thidwick the Big-Hearted Moose
Yertle the Turtle and other stories